*For all the little people taking on
the big problems—Kate, Jol, Terri*

First American Edition 2021
Kane Miller, A Division of EDC Publishing

Text copyright © Kate and Jol Temple, 2021
Illustrations copyright © Terri Rose Baynton, 2021

First published by Scholastic Press, a division of Scholastic Australia Pty Limited in 2021.
This edition published under license from Scholastic Australia Pty Limited.

For information contact:
Kane Miller, A Division of EDC Publishing
5402 S 122nd E Ave, Tulsa, OK 74146
www.kanemiller.com
www.myubam.com

Library of Congress Control Number: 2020949697
Printed in China
2 3 4 5 6 7 8 9 10
ISBN: 978-1-68464-293-9

Move that Mountain

There are two sides to every story

Kate & Jol Temple

Terri Rose Baynton

Kane Miller
A DIVISION OF EDC PUBLISHING

We *can't* move
that mountain

So it's
madness to think

We can make it budge

We can make it shrink

The problem's *too big*

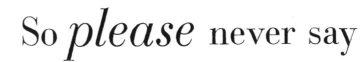

So *please* never say

If we all work
together

We *will* find a way

1, 2, 3,
HEAVE!

If we can't move it now

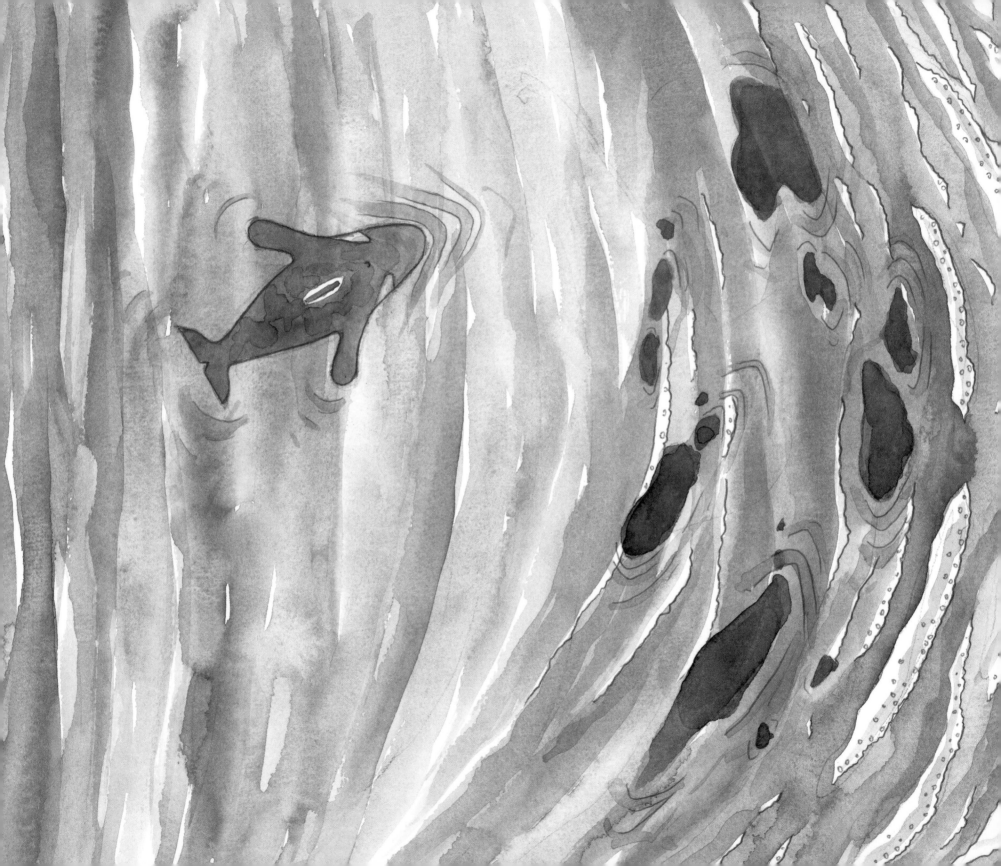

It *won't*
move at all

We *must*
face facts

We're *far, far*
too small

So let's *never* believe

We can move mountains

We can move mountains, if we all *play our part.*
Just read it again, from the back to the start.